T0365177

SOLDIER CRAB, MONKEY & ALL AH WE

Written by
C. N. Lawrence

Illustrated by
Susan Shorter

AuthorHouse™
1663 Liberty Drive
Bloomington, IN 47403
www.authorhouse.com
Phone: 833-262-8899

Because of the dynamic nature of the Internet, any web addresses or links contained in this book may have changed
since publication and may no longer be valid. The views expressed in this work are solely those of the author and do
not necessarily reflect the views of the publisher, and the publisher hereby disclaims any responsibility for them.

Any people depicted in stock imagery provided by Getty Images are models,
and such images are being used for illustrative purposes only.
Certain stock imagery © Getty Images.

This book is printed on acid-free paper.

ISBN: 978-1-4918-4739-8 (sc)
ISBN: 978-1-4918-4740-4 (e)

Library of Congress Control Number: 2014900255

Print information available on the last page.

Published by AuthorHouse 11/30/2023

authorHOUSE

Table of Contents

Dedication

To my favorite son, Davidson,
my favorite daughter, Carlina
and to my grandsons, Z'Kai, David, Xavier and Z'yirh.
I am thankful to God for courage, my family and friends
for their support and encouragement especially, Claudius.

Wild, Wild Nevis Donkey

Sleepy is a handsome, strong Nevisian donkey. Once upon a time his parents were high ranking donkeys among the Gingerland donkey clans many years ago.

2

Nevisian donkeys were loyal to their masters; carrying all their heavy loads of sticks, ground provision, and hog-meat (scrap vegetation), bags of coals and whatever else was placed upon their backs.

4

Thirty years ago, Donkeys were the transportation of choice on the island; taking Nevisians on their journeys wherever they were going: to market, church, town, to the mountain, even Sunday visiting to hang with friends.

But that was life on Nevis long ago. Nevis has changed and has become "modern", so nobody wants donkeys anymore and poor Sleepy and his family are abandoned, unwanted, left to graze the pastures of Nevis.

This makes Sleepy very sad because he and his family are not wanted anymore.

Everyone has cars now or take the to public bus. Nevis donkeys just get chased away now. They are blamed for overturning garbage bins and eating all the good pasture grass that the other "useful" livestock animals need.

Isn't the Nevisian donkey Nevisian anymore?

They are so wild now, but years ago Nevisian people would walk for miles to find their lost donkey.

"What is the future of the Nevisian donkey?" Sleepy wondered. "We have made our contribution to society but now we are no longer wanted."

Poor Nevisian donkey wild, wild and unwanted.

10

Kendra's Discovery

Little Kendra and her mom were walking down Westbury Road; she was very excited to go to town with her mother. As they walked Kendra noticed everything— the birds, butterflies and flowers.

Suddenly, something grabbed her attention. She noticed something brown and fuzzy dashing across the road.

"What was that mommy?" Kendra asked. "What was what?" her mother asked.

"Look!" "There goes another one!" And as her mother looked in the direction Kendra was pointing, she noticed a family of mongoose.

The mother mongoose was leading her little ones across the road and into the nearby bushes. The mother mongoose looked nervous as she did her best to keep her young ones together and get them to safety.

"Mommy, there are so many of them," Kendra said, "what are they?" "I have never seen them before." "Oh Kendra, it's okay, these are just Nevisian Mongoose." "When I was a little girl we use to see them cross the roads all the time, they always seem to be in a hurry to get to where they are going."

14

"My mother, your grandmother, told me that mongooses were brought to Nevis to control the snake population on the island many years ago."

"Nevis has snakes?" Kendra asked. "No dear, not anymore, thanks to the mongoose; they are great hunters." "So now we don't have to worry about harmful snakes anymore and you can play outside without me worrying about you being bitten by a snake."

"What about the mongoose?" Kendra asked, "will they bite while I'm out playing?" "No darling, mongoose usually stay away from people and now that you mention it, we hardly see mongooses anymore, it seem like we are losing the Nevisian mongoose too," mother said.

"I hope that's not true", said Kendra, "they are so cute looking." "I hope we never lose the mongoose," as she and her mother boarded the bus for town.

Island Style Granny Stories

Life on the tiny Caribbean island of Nevis about thirty years ago was simple and what granny said was true. Listen to these island stories that Granny liked to tell and decide if they are true.

Children are playing outside, running and laughing with their friends. Adults are cooking, cleaning and looking after the home. Suddenly a bumblebee comes out of nowhere and buzzes around their heads...the children scream thinking the bee may sting, but granny smiles and says, "don't worry it won't sting; the bumblebee is just bringing us a message, for very soon we will receive a letter with a piece of money in it and good news from afar."

Granny's second story is even more interesting.... It's Saturday evening and Granny and Poppy are taking a break after a day of hard work. Poppy was sitting on the doorstep while Granny was lying down on the floor of the house; they were discussing the day's events, then all of a sudden a rooster stands right in-front of the house door and crows, "cock-a-doodle-do." The children began to pay attention because Granny did not shew away the rooster, instead she got up and said, "Poppy you have to get that broken window fixed because visitors are coming!" That's what it means when the rooster crows in front of the house door like that! Granny made such a fuss that Poppy had to get up right away and got to work making the repairs.

The next story Granny tells is the one that amaze me the most. Granny asked the children, "you notice how all around Nevis you see goats trying to climb trees?" "Yes" said the children. "Well why do you think those goats do that?" "Sheep don't do it, donkeys don't do it.... goats are the only animal you see with almost its entire body up in a tree while dining on the green delicious leaves."

"This my dear children is because the Nevis vervet monkey once upon a time, long, long ago had an unusual relationship with the goat."

"They got along very well, they were very good friends, so the monkey decided one day that he was going to teach his friend the goat how to climb just like the monkey could climb."

"But something went terribly wrong along the way and there was a falling out between the goat and the monkey, so then the goat decided to teach dogs how to climb just as the monkey was teaching the goat." And children, we all know that dogs and monkeys are fierce enemies.

Dogs would catch and eat monkeys if they were hungry enough; this was not good news for the monkey.

"When the monkey found out that the goat was teaching the dog everything that monkey was teaching them about climbing, monkey immediately stopped all climbing lessons to the goat."

"So you see my dear children, why it is that goats can only go halfway up a tree?" "Yes Granny we understand but how do you know so many things?"

"Well my sweet children, my grandmother told me all these stories when I was little, just like I am telling you today and someday you will tell your children." "Hopefully they would enjoy the Nevisian stories just as much."

28

Pet Soldier Crabs?

For many years soldier crabs have been feared by children because of their very sharp pinchers.

No one had use for these crabs; they are not edible, they move slowly and they are kind of creepy looking.

There was no fun in these crabs, nothing special about them at all... absolutely nothing.

Until a very adventurous boy named Kai came along, Kai was a very active 5 year old who was always on the go. He loved to run and play every chance he got.

Kai loves animals of all sorts, and the first time he saw a soldier crab, he wanted one for a pet.

Everyone tried to tell Kai that the crabs were dangerous and would pinch him if he touched them; he was warned that these soldier crabs cannot be a boys pet!

29

But Kai could not be convinced and set out with a small pail to hunt soldier crabs around his yard, but he could not find any crabs.

Kai did not give up, he begged his mom to take him hunting for crabs in the ghaut near his house but she said "no" "those crabs are dangerous and cannot be pets." So Kai set out to find someone else that would take him crab hunting. He found his cousin Jomo and asked Jomo to take him to the ghaut to hunt for soldier crabs and Jomo said "yes!"

So Kai, with his pail and his cousin Jomo, set out for the nearby ghaut to go soldier crab hunting.

After a while Kai came running to his mother, "look, look I have crabs, lots of them!" When his mother looked into his pail, she was amazed to see how many crabs Kai had in his bucket... "Jomo helped me find them he exclaimed with excitement!"

There were some big ones, and some small ones. Kai's mom asked him, "what are you going to do with all those crabs?"

"Keep them," Kai said. "What are you going to feed them, do you know what soldier crabs eat?"

"Grass!" Said Kai, so Kai began to pick green grass to put into the bucket for his crabs. His mom asked, "How do you know they eat grass?" "Yes, yes," he said, "they eat grass."

Kai wanted to bring his pail of crabs into the house but his mom did not let him. His mom tried to convince him to set the crabs free but Kai begged and begged until his mom gave in and allowed him to let the crabs stay on the porch.

Everyone in the village thought this little boy was strange to have soldier crabs for his pet. The villagers would all ask, "what are you going to do with them?" "Keep them, they are my pets," Kai would reply.

The older men in the village would warn him that the crabs would pinch him; they all told him to be careful.

But Kai amazed everyone with his crabs; he played with his crabs. He would hold them in the palm of his hand and the crabs would march in his palms and did not pinch him with their pinchers.

He fed them with grass and sugar apples and gave them water. Kai was the first and only boy to have soldier crabs as pets!

Other children in the village began wanting soldier crabs for their pets too, so Kai was able to make the soldier crab interesting and useful to others.

Consequently, Kai and his friends from the village all went soldier crab hunting together with their pails to catch more soldier crabs. Now all the boys in the village had soldier crabs for pets and Kai was very happy

The End.

Garbage on an Island

Nat is a boy who lives on an island located in the Caribbean Sea. Nat's island is very small, only 36 square miles with 12,000 people living there.

There is a huge mountain in the middle of the island that is over 3000 feet tall!

Nat thought his island was the most beautiful of all the Caribbean islands. He saw pictures of the other islands on TV and in books he had read but Nat always declared that his island is the best.

But there is a problem about his island that bothered Nat from time to time and Nat thought that this problem could change his island from being the most beautiful.

Nat's concern was about garbage and litter on his island.

Nat often wondered...how does a small island in the middle of the ocean get rid of its garbage?

Huge ships and planes bring all sorts of products made in many countries around the world to Nat's island because people want these things. His mother told him that these are "consumer items."

But Nat being his usual curious self began to wonder what happens to all these things that the ships and planes bring, when they are broken, old, and no longer useful.

Nat was paying close attention and was always asking the adults in his life questions about the garbage problem...how does an island get rid of its garbage he would ask?

One day, on his way to the beach in the family car, they drove pass an old refrigerator in the grass on the side of the road.

This caused Nat to remember the old abandoned car that he sees in the pasture each day when he is on the school bus going to school.

Nat was deep in thought and wondered about the litter he saw along the road side and just as he was about to ask his Dad where does garbage on the island go, a jeep zoomed by and the driver tossed a soda can out of the window.

Nat wondered and thought and finally said, "Dad I think I know, I think I have the answer..." "Answer to what son?" his father asked. "The answer to the problem of what happens to garbage and litter on an island."

His dad wanted to hear what Nat had to say about the issue of garbage on the island so he turned down the volume on the car radio and said "tell me son because we really need to work on this together."

Nat took a deep breath and said, "well, Dad...I see the ships and planes bringing things mom calls **goods** to our island but I don't see them taking anything back with them when they leave, so I know our garbage is not leaving the island on ships and planes."

"And we do not have any factories here on our island, so we are not making new things from old things that people don't want any more and throw out."

"Visitors come from all around the world to take their vacations here and swim in our beaches. Some of them even come back every year, so we cannot put the garbage in the sea either."

"The garbage truck comes to our house to empty the garbage bin every week but what do they do with all the garbage they collect?"

"My teacher told us at school to tell our parents to reduce, reuse and recycle, so that there would be less garbage to put out, but they don't seem to be listening to us."

"Son, you still have not told me yet where you think the garbage goes." "You know what I think dad?" "The garbage truck picks up the garbage from all the homes on the island and then they drive all the way up to the top of the mountain peak and dump it all in the big opening at the top of the 'mountain!"

"That must be it Dad because what else can people living on an island do with all the garbage they create?" "Taking it all to the top of the mountain will surely solve the problem, Nat insisted; how else do you keep an island clean?"

"The old car and refrigerator must be waiting to be picked up and taken to the top of the Peak and dropped in the big opening at the top; so it all can disappear from our sight."

Nat's father "chuckled", but when he realized how serious his son was about this problem of garbage on the island and how much he wants to solve the problem, he explained to him that until everyone got as serious and as concerned as Nat is about the problem the issue of garbage and litter will not go away.

"We cannot put the garbage into the crater of the mountain my son but if we all took responsibility and reduce, reuse and recycle as much as possible it would make a big difference especially on an island like ours."

"Perhaps one day soon we will see those ships and planes carry old things away from our island just as they bring new things each week."

"We love it when people come from around the world to visit our island; we are happy to show them everything our island has to offer, and one day Nat, with the help of you, your friends, and everyone living here, we will show our visitors exactly how we keep an island clean."

Nat said to his Dad, "I have already started... I do not litter and I asked mom to let me give my toys, clothes and books that I no longer want to charity."

"I am proud of you son, that will certainly help."

About the Author:

C.N. Lawrence was born on the island of Nevis in the Caribbean; she also lived on the island of St. Croix, U.S.V.I. She has two adult children and four grandchildren and makes her home on Nevis.

Printed in the United States
by Baker & Taylor Publisher Services